The authors extend heartfelt thanks to Sarah Greene, Naimy Hackett, Andrew Appel, Daniela Achille, Professor Cesarino Ruini and the Emilia-Romagna Museums Directorate, as well as Ted Chapin, Dana Siegel, and The Rodgers & Hammerstein Organization.

ABOUT THIS BOOK

The illustrations for this book were done in mixed media (watercolor, gouache, colored pencils) on Arches Paper (100% cotton 300 gr). This book was edited by Lisa Yoskowitz and designed by Véronique Lefèvre Sweet. The production was supervised by Kimberly Stella, and the production editor was Annie McDonnell. The text was set in Adobe Jenson Pro Regular, and the display type is Windlass Lowercase regular.

THE FIRST NOTES

The Story of DO, RE, MI

By **Julie Andrews** *&* **Emma Walton Hamilton**

Art by **Chiara Fedele**

L B

Little, Brown and Company

New York Boston

Dear Reader,

"Let's start at the very beginning . . .
a very good place to start.

When you read, you begin with A-B-C.
When you sing, you begin with Do-Re-Mi."

These are the first words of a famous song from a musical called *The Sound of Music.* Maybe you know the part of the song that goes like this:

"Doe, a deer, a female deer,
Ray, a drop of golden sun,
Me, a name I call myself,
Far, a long, long way to run . . ."

The song teaches us the names of the notes that make up our musical scale:

Do, Re, Mi, Fa, Sol, La, and *Ti.*

Together, they are called *Solfège* (pronounced sol-fej). Whether you play these notes on an instrument or simply sing them, their names are always the same. They are the building blocks of how we learn music.

There was a time when no one knew how to read or write music. The only way to learn a song was to hear it sung by someone else and then remember it. This made things very confusing, since people's memories were not always reliable. But in those days no one had a better way to teach music.

This book was inspired by the true story of one dedicated monk, who loved music so much that he invented a new way to teach it . . . and changed the way we understand music today.

Julie Andrews & Emma Walton Hamilton

A thousand years ago, in the small community of Pomposa, Italy, a boy named Guido was sent to a monastery to begin his schooling. In those days, a monastery was considered the best place to receive an education. The monks who lived and taught there were studious and wise.

Young Guido spent his days learning Latin, math, astronomy, and his favorite subject, music. He heard music everywhere . . . in the warm voices of the monks chanting their prayers and in the chiming of the bells that summoned them to chapel several times a day.

He heard it in the sounds of nature . . .
in the splish-splashing of the stream where
he fished with his friend Brother Michael;
in the buzz and hum of bees and crickets
in the monastery garden; and in the lilting
song of the nightingale that lulled him to
sleep at night.

Guido yearned to know everything about music and dreamed of one day teaching it to others. But learning music was *hard*. Day after day, week after week, Guido listened, memorized, and practiced— knowing it could take ten years to master the complicated hymns and harmonies he loved so much.

When he wasn't studying, Guido worked in the monastery's great library.

He often wondered why music couldn't be written down and read like words in books.

Guido thought about this a lot. One day, while practicing his hymns, he made a discovery: He was only singing *six* basic tones. No matter how high or low he sang, no matter what melody, the same tones repeated themselves!

He found a piece of parchment and made a small mark on it to represent the lowest tone. Then he drew another, and another—stacking each mark higher than the next, just as he had been singing them. His heart beat faster as he drew lines between and through the marks, as if they were climbing a ladder.

Could *this* be a way to write music?

If so, then each of the six marks would need a name. Humming his favorite hymn, he noticed that it, too, had six parts.

Ut queant laxis
resonare fibris
mira gestorum
famuli tuorum
Solvi polluti
labii reatum

He took the first syllable from each line of his hymn and noted it next to one of the marks he had made on the parchment, going from the bottom to the top.

la

sol

fa

mi

re

ut

He sang each syllable aloud, raising his voice step by step to match the way the notes marched up the lines.

Guido thought he might burst with excitement! If all the chants, all the hymns, all the harmonies could be written down in this way, maybe people could learn to *read* music. Then they would always know the correct melody to sing, even if they had never heard it before!

Clutching his parchment to his chest, he raced across the courtyard to share his discovery with his teachers. But the monks simply shrugged and turned back to their work. They had no interest in trying something new. One even suggested that Guido should spend less time thinking up foolish ideas and more time praying.

Heavy-hearted, Guido trudged back to his chamber.

In the days that followed, Guido grew despondent. Instead of fishing and gardening, instead of singing and enjoying all the sounds of music around him, he kept to himself . . . and his world became quiet.

One day, a visitor arrived at the monastery. Bishop Theodald of Arezzo was searching for a teacher to train the choir singers at his great cathedral. The bishop had heard of Guido's passion for music and invited him to take the position. Guido quickly accepted.

Guido left Pomposa and began the journey to his new
home. The sun warmed his back, songbirds twittered, and the
clip-clopping of his donkey's hooves made a happy rhythm as
he jogged along. A breeze whispered through the olive trees,
and the tall cypresses stood to attention. Guido began to hum
. . . and then, to sing.

Bishop Theodald welcomed Guido, and when the young monk shared his musical ideas, the bishop did not shrug or turn away. He clapped his hands in delight and encouraged Guido to teach this new method to his cathedral singers.

As Guido worked with his pupils, he sometimes pointed to his hand, where he had written the musical notes.

Within days, the choir had mastered hymns they had never heard before! Amazed, the bishop urged Guido to write a book about his revolutionary ideas. Guido dedicated his book to the kindly bishop.

Word of Guido's innovative approach to teaching
music began to spread far and wide.

Early one morning, the clatter of hooves and a fanfare of
trumpets resounded through the Grande Piazza of Arezzo.
Sleepy villagers tumbled out of their homes to see what the
commotion was about.

Three magnificently robed cardinals carried a message from Pope John XIX, the most important leader in the land. The pope had heard of Guido's musical theories, and he was summoning the young monk to Rome so he could see them for himself.

The pope immersed himself in Guido's ideas and was so impressed by the ease with which he was able to learn new melodies that he suggested Guido stay in Rome permanently to teach the Roman clergy.

But Guido politely declined the pope's offer. Though honored by the invitation, he preferred to return to his simple, pastoral life in Arezzo.

It is said that on his way home, Guido stopped at the monastery in Pomposa, where the monks who had been so disagreeable now welcomed him and apologized sincerely for their lack of faith in him. Guido surely would have forgiven them—grateful to have realized his dream of teaching music and to have made its joys easier for people to learn.

Guido's system of musical notation, now called Solfège, eventually spread throughout Europe and across the world.

Many years later, Guido's square notes became oval shapes; the first note, "Ut," was changed to "Do," and a seventh note—"Ti"—was added, to become the musical scale we know and use today, and the basis for the song "Do-Re-Mi."

Imagine if Guido could have heard that famous song! What fun he might have had singing it with his students . . .

"Doe, a deer, a female deer,

Ray, a drop of golden sun,

"Me, a name I call myself,

Far, a long, long way to run,

"Sew, a needle pulling thread,

La, a note to follow Sew,

"Tea, a drink with jam and bread,

That will bring us back to Doe!
Do-Re-Mi-Fa-Sol-La-Ti-Do!"

A Note About the Song "Do-Re-Mi"

The song "Do-Re-Mi" was written by two famous gentlemen, Richard Rodgers and Oscar Hammerstein, for their show *The Sound of Music*, based on the true story of an Austrian woman named Maria von Trapp. She became governess to seven children who had recently lost their mother and brought joy back to their lives by teaching them about music. Later, she married their father, and the family became a well-known singing group called the Trapp Family Singers.

I was fortunate to play the part of Maria in the film version of *The Sound of Music*. I didn't know about Guido's invention of the musical scale—now called Solfège—when I first sang "Do-Re-Mi" in the film. Maria uses the song to teach the von Trapp children the basics of music, saying "When you know the notes to sing, you can sing most anything!" I like to think that Messrs. Rodgers and Hammerstein researched Guido's theories when writing their song. How clever of them to turn Guido's teachings into a song so memorable and accessible that it remains a popular way to introduce children to music today.

These two gifted gentlemen wrote a number of magnificent musicals and songs, together and apart. Mr. Rodgers wrote the music, and Mr. Hammerstein wrote the words—or lyrics. I've had the pleasure of singing many of their songs over the years. The melodies are always beautiful, and the words are clear and meaningful, making them a joy to sing.

If you are interested in music, you cannot go wrong listening to the works of Rodgers and Hammerstein, which in addition to *The Sound of Music* include such classics as *Oklahoma*, *Carousel*, *South Pacific*, and *The King and I*, among many others. Rodgers and Hammerstein were truly giants in their field, and I am so grateful to have known and worked with them.

Julie Andrews

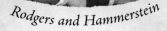

Rodgers and Hammerstein

Glossary

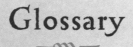

- **BISHOP:** a high-ranking Christian priest, in charge of all the churches and priests within his district.

- **CARDINAL:** a powerful bishop who is appointed by, and serves as an advisor to, the pope. Cardinals assist in the governance of the Catholic Church. They usually wear distinctive red robes and a special hat.

- **CATHEDRAL:** the largest and most important church in a Christian diocese, or district, run by the bishop of that district.

- **CHANT/CHANTING:** a type of religious singing, usually unaccompanied, consisting of simple, repeated tones and words and sung as an aid to prayer.

- **CHOIR:** a group of singers who perform together. In Guido's time, choirs were usually all male and associated with a specific church or cathedral.

- **CLERGY:** the leaders of a specific religion or religious group. The Christian clergy is comprised of deacons, priests, bishops, cardinals, and popes.

- **FANFARE:** a brief musical "announcement," usually played on brass instruments, to introduce someone or something important.

- **HARMONY/HARMONIES:** a combination of musical tones sung or played together to make a pleasing sound.

- **HYMN:** a poetic and spiritual song, used to praise God and other religious figures.

- **MELODY:** a sequence of notes that make a pattern we can hear and recognize.

- **MONASTERY:** a building or group of buildings in which monks live, work, and worship.

- **MONK:** a man who has devoted himself entirely to his religion. Monks live alone or with a group of other monks, and dedicate themselves to prayer and service. A female monk is called a nun.

- **MUSICAL:** 1) relating to music or having a pleasing sound, or 2) a play or film including music and songs.

- **NOTATION/MUSICAL NOTATION:** the art of writing music down so that it can be read and played. A rough form of musical notation, called neumes, did exist before Guido's time. It consisted of symbols that represented in general terms how music was "kind of" supposed to sound. Guido's system assured consistency with respect to the pitch and sound of all notes in a clear and reliable way. It changed forever how music was taught and preserved.

- **NOTE/MUSICAL NOTE:** a written symbol that represents a certain musical tone or sound. In Guido's time, musical notes were drawn as squares—today, we use ovals to depict them.

- **PARCHMENT:** before the existence of paper, people wrote on parchment. It was made from dried and flattened animal skins and was expensive and hard to come by.

- **PIAZZA:** an open public space, or square, in an Italian town or city.

- **POPE:** the head of the Catholic Church. The word comes from the Latin term for "father." The pope lives in Rome, Italy, in a place called Vatican City.

- **SCALE/MUSICAL SCALE:** a set of musical notes in an ordered sequence. The Western musical scale is comprised of seven consecutive notes—A, B, C, D, E, F, and G—each note higher than the last. Once completed, the scale can be repeated, climbing progressively as it goes. The distance between two of the same notes (such as middle C and the next C above it) is called an octave.

- **SOLFÈGE:** the sequence of seven syllables—Do, Re, Mi, Fa, Sol, La, and Ti—originally devised by Guido d'Arezzo and still used today to teach music. Each syllable represents one of the seven notes on the musical scale and allows a musician to "hear" the pitch or sound that the written music requires.

- **TONE:** the quality of sound made when a musical note is played or sung.

A Day in Guido's Life at Pomposa Abbey

Guido d'Arezzo belonged to the Benedictine order of monks, named for Saint Benedict, who in the fifth century founded multiple monasteries in Italy. Benedictine monks lived simple lives, devoting themselves to God and to serving others. Because they all lived together in the same way, they called one another "brothers" and followed "The Rule of Saint Benedict," which organized the day into regular periods of prayer, study, work, and sleep.

Guido's day typically began at two AM, when the church bell chimed to announce the first prayers, or Matins. The monks would leave their dormitories, where they slept on straw pallets, and go to the chapel to chant. In the winter, they might return to bed afterward and sleep for a few more hours, until Lauds—the dawn songs of praise and thanks—but in the summer, they often stayed awake, continuing to sing, pray, read, or work through the darkest hours until dawn.

The younger monks spent the morning hours studying their lessons. Lunch was the main meal of the day and typically consisted of bread, vegetables, fruit, eggs, cheese, and fish. After lunch, the monks "rested" for a while by walking in the inner courtyard, usually under porticos that protected them from sun and bad weather. This was one of the few times in the day when they were allowed to speak to one another, as conversation was not permitted in church or at mealtimes . . . but any discussion was expected to be thoughtful and mostly devoted to religious matters.

In the afternoons, the monks did manual labor. Some tended the fields or gardens, harvesting the fruits, vegetables, and herbs they grew; others cared for the livestock. Still others cooked or did laundry, carpentry, sewing, and repairs. Some of the older monks made wine and herbal medicines, and others copied and illustrated ancient manuscripts and sacred texts by hand in the library, known as the scriptorium.

Afternoon work was interrupted twice daily for more prayers and chanting. Benedictine monks spent an average of six to eight hours a day in prayer. The early evening prayers, called Vespers, took place at sunset, along with "the lighting of the lamps" (candles, as they had no electricity). The monks then ate a simple dinner, while listening to one of the brothers read from a sacred text. After the Compline—the final prayer of the evening—the monks retired to bed early, usually as soon as it was dark.

Medieval monks had few possessions and wore simple woolen tunics, tied at the waist with a belt made of rope, often covered by another robe with a deep hood, called a cowl. When a monk joined the brotherhood, he shaved the top of his head to create a crown effect, as a symbol of his devotion to God and his willingness to give up all forms of vanity.

Monks were very important to their community. In addition to educating youth, they cared for the poor, the sick, and the aged. Travelers could always find a good meal and accommodation at a monastery. Monks were also patrons of the arts, sponsoring artists and architects to design and embellish their buildings and churches. Finally, they were the keepers of history, collecting important books, letters, and biographies in their extensive libraries.

Benedictine monks still exist around the world today, and their daily routines remain much the same as they were in Guido's time, a thousand years ago.

The Guidonian Hand

—ᴍ—

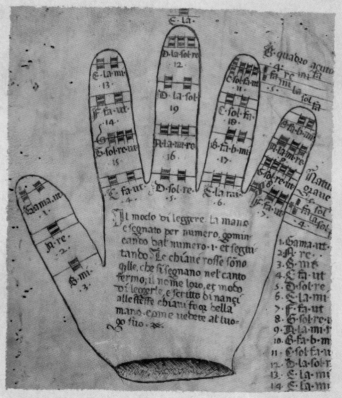

Using the hand to help teach music was not invented by Guido, but he did assign musical notes to each finger and joint, just as he had drawn them on his parchment—perhaps because parchment was so hard to come by. By pointing to his hand while teaching, Guido gave his students a way of visualizing the relationship of one note to another that they could carry with them anywhere. This resulted in the "Guidonian Hand" being named after him. Music instructors throughout the Middle Ages considered this method one of the best ways to teach sight-singing.

Guidonian Hand from a manuscript from Mantua, last quarter of the 15th century (Oxford University MS Canon. Liturg. 216. f.168 recto) (Bodleian Library)

A Historical Note

While not many specifics of Guido's life are well documented, our research confirms the following:

- He lived during the first part of the eleventh century and is widely considered to be the father of modern musical notation.

- He was educated and trained as a Benedictine monk at Pomposa Abbey on the Adriatic coast, in what was then the Po Delta but is now the Emilia-Romagna region of Italy. The abbey was famous for its collection of important manuscripts.

- Guido loved music and wanted to find a better way to teach it to others.

- His best friend was a monk named Brother Michael.

- He created the "Do-Re-Mi" Solfège by using the first syllables of each line in a hymn called "*Ut queant laxis*."

- His musical ideas were not well received by his fellow monks.

- He was invited to move to Arezzo by Bishop Theodald and taught his theories to the choir at the cathedral there.

- He wrote and published *Micrologus*, a treatise on medieval music, in approximately 1026 and dedicated it to the Bishop of Arezzo.

- Word of his techniques spread to Rome, and Pope John XIX invited him to the Vatican so he could study Guido's work for himself.

- The pope asked him to stay in Rome, but Guido declined, possibly due to ill health.

- His musical theories spread across Europe and elsewhere and remain in use today.

Some of these facts are confirmed in Guido's "Letter to Brother Michael Concerning How to Sing an Unknown Chant," written in 1033. Others were confirmed by historical advisor Professor Cesarino Ruini and the Emilia-Romagna Museums Directorate.

For music lovers everywhere —J.A. and E.W.H.

To my beloved dad —C.F.

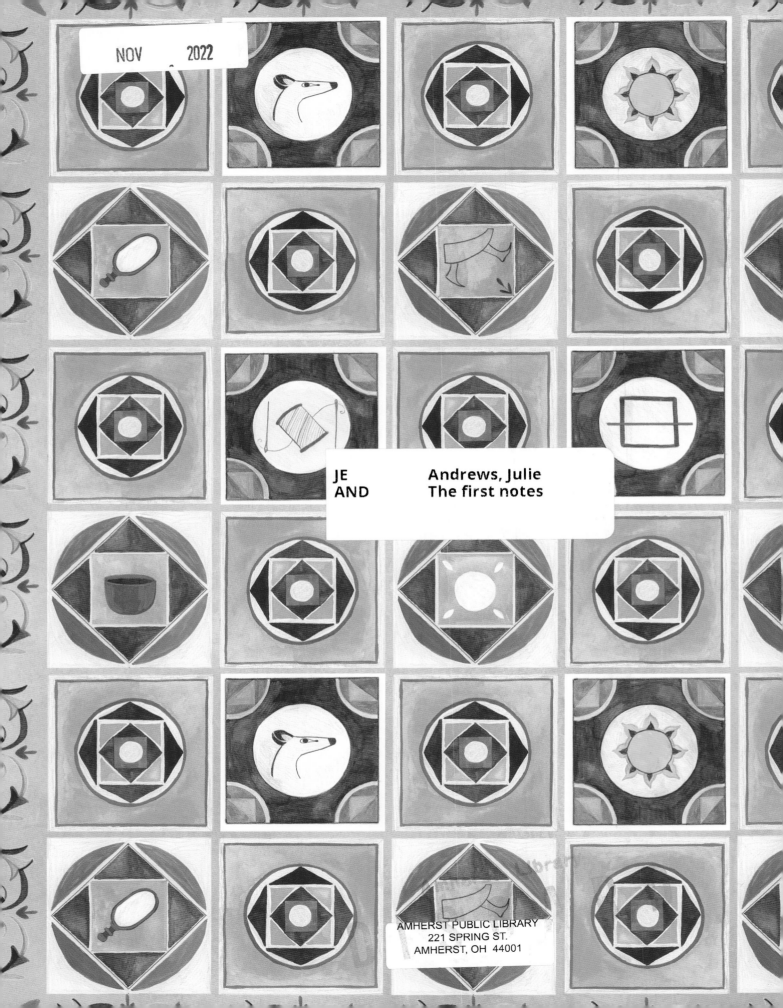